the witch princess

GHOST SHIP

THE SUNKEN KINGDOM 1

GHOST SHIP

by Kim Wilkins

illustrated by D. M. Cornish

Random House New York

Text copyright © 2006 by Kim Wilkins
Illustrations copyright © 2006 by D. M. Cornish

Published in the United States by Random House Children's Books,
a division of Random House, Inc., New York. Originally published
in Australia by Omnibus Books, an imprint
of Scholastic Australia Pty. Ltd., Gosford, in 2006.

Random House and colophon are registered trademarks of
Random House, Inc.

Visit us on the Web!
www.randomhouse.com/kids

Educators and librarians, for a variety of teaching tools, visit us at
www.randomhouse.com/teachers

Library of Congress Cataloging-in-Publication Data
Wilkins, Kim.
Ghost ship / by Kim Wilkins ; illustrated by D. M. Cornish. — 1st ed.
      p.   cm. — (The sunken kingdom ; bk. 1)
Summary: After their parents, the rulers of the Star Lands, are
deposed and their kingdom flooded, Asa and Rollo hide out until
they come into possession of a ghost ship and magic powers, which
they use to find the baby sister they thought had died with their
parents.
ISBN 978-0-375-84806-3 (pbk.) —
ISBN 978-0-375-94806-0 (lib. bdg.)
[1. Brothers and sisters—Fiction. 2. Fantasy.] I. Cornish, D. M.
(David M.), ill. II. Title.
PZ7.W64867Gh 2008
[Fic]—dc22   2007027729

PRINTED IN MALAYSIA
10 9 8 7 6 5 4 3 2 1
First Edition

Random House Children's Books supports the First Amendment
and celebrates the right to read.

For Luka

CONTENTS

CHAPTER 1

AN UNEXPECTED VISITOR

"Asa! Sky patrol!"

Asa's heart jumped. She leapt to her feet and glanced up the muddy slope at her younger brother, Rollo, who waved madly and pointed at the sky.

"I'm coming!" she yelled, pocketing in her damp skirt the colored stones she had been collecting. She sped away from the mud, up the slope, and onto the grass. A gull swooped overhead, and the heavy salt smell of the sea stuck to her clothes. Breathless, she grabbed Rollo's hand and kept running.

"Up there!" he said, and now Asa could see it on the horizon. A black shape against the pale morning sky: one of Emperor Flood's fleet of balloons. They patrolled the skies, looking for traitors, searching out supporters of the deposed royal family. Especially the two remaining children of the royal family: Asa and Rollo.

They hurried up the hill, the grass scratchy under their bare feet.

"It's coming too fast," Asa said. "We'll never make it back to Two Hills Keep."

"The cave, then," Rollo said.

The cave. How she hated it. It smelled like fish and seaweed, and reminded her of the night Emperor Flood's evil magic had swollen the sea, sinking her parents' kingdom, the Star Lands. That awful night, she and Rollo had hidden in the cave for hours. When they emerged, their parents—King Sigurd and the Star Queen—were dead, along with their baby sister, Una. The cave had once been their favorite place to play,

high up in a cliff overlooking the Great Sea, hidden under the branches of a huge sea willow. Now the water lapped at its entrance, and the branches of the sea willow soaked their drooping tips at high tide.

Asa didn't want to go back to the cave. But the black shape loomed closer. She could hear the hiss of the balloon approaching.

"All right," she said, squeezing Rollo's hand. "The cave."

They changed direction, scrambling across the slope and down, and the sea willow came into view, its long silvery branches catching the early-morning light.

"Hurry," she said, pushing Rollo ahead. He scurried farther down the slope, over rocks and loose ground. Asa's blood pounded. She risked a look back. The black half-moon of the balloon's top was rising behind the slope. She slid on the loose ground, caught herself on a rock. A hot pain. The jagged edge of the rock had split open her palm. She clutched it with her other hand and blood oozed between her fingers. Nursing the injury against her chest, she found her way to the cave.

"Asa, you're bleeding," Rollo said as she landed next to him.

She tore a strip off the bottom of her skirt and wrapped her palm in it. Wincing, she tied the knot with her teeth. But this was no time for tears or complaining. "Hush, now," she said, catching her breath. "Quiet and still."

For a few long moments, all she could hear was their ragged breathing, the pull of the sea, the distant cries of gulls. But then, the familiar hiss as the balloon filled with hot air.

Sssshhhhhhhhhhhhhhhhhhhh.

The sound of giant, evil lungs drawing sickly breath.

Asa and Rollo pressed themselves against the back wall of the cave. Asa's heartbeat was loud in her ears.

Sssshhhhhhhhhhhhhhhhhhhh.

It was coming closer. She drew up her feet so her knees were right against her chest. Rollo pressed his face into her side and his fair hair fell forward. She slid her arm around him, her eyes wide and watching the entrance.

A black shape descended behind the twisted branches of the sea willow. It was the bottom edge of the spy-seat: the square basket that hung from the balloon. She knew that Flood's spies would be sitting in the spy-seat, with their compasses and brass telescopes and gleaming knives. The balloon only had to descend another two feet and the spies would be staring straight into the cave. She pushed herself against the cave wall, but couldn't shrink back any farther. Her heart thundered in her ears. "Please, please," she whispered, over and over, silently. Rollo pressed himself against her harder, his hot little hand clutching her injured palm. Sweat made the wound sting.

The basket lifted again and disappeared from sight. *Sssshhhhhhhhhhhhhhhhhhhh.*

Up it went. Asa breathed. Rollo lifted his head. She put her finger to her lips to remind him to stay quiet a little longer.

Then the hissing began once more. The balloon was withdrawing, taking off over the sunken kingdom, searching elsewhere for traitors and royalists.

Rollo smiled. "It's gone."

"Let's get home," Asa said, standing on shaky legs.

"I wasn't really afraid," Rollo said with a grin.

"Yes, you were."

"No, I wasn't."

They emerged into the pale morning light and Asa led the way home.

Asa and Rollo lived with their aunt Katla at Two Hills Keep. Although the Keep looked like a tiny cottage built of mud and grass, it was actually far larger and concealed an underground maze of secret rooms. The King and Queen had it built when Asa was born, just in case their children were ever in danger and needed to hide. It came into view above the rise. Wildflowers grew over the grassy walls and a drooping tree disguised it almost entirely. In the year since Emperor Flood had killed their family and taken over the land, he had never managed to find them here.

"Who's that?" Rollo said, pointing across the field.

Asa noticed it at the same time: an old man with his left arm pinned to his chest paced near the front entrance of the Keep.

"I don't know," she said warily, slowing her pace.

Rollo pulled up. "What if he's a spy?"

Asa didn't know what to do. She had never seen the strange man before, but he looked like he was waiting for them.

At that moment, Katla emerged and spotted them. She beckoned anxiously. "Come quickly, children," she called. "You have a special visitor."

The children hurried over as the old man turned to watch them. Asa didn't like his steely eyes, his hooked nose, or the cruel set of his mouth. Something about him made her skin prickle. A cool gust of morning air shivered over her. The wound on her hand had begun to throb lightly.

"Asa, Rollo," Katla said stiffly, "I want you to meet Egil Cripplehand." Katla glanced at him nervously, then back to the children. "He has news of your sister."

"Una?" Rollo said, puzzled.

The stranger fixed him with a stony gaze. "She's alive," he said. "Your sister is alive."

CHAPTER 2

EGIL CRIPPLEHAND'S TALE

Egil Cripplehand wouldn't say another word until they were safely in the Keep, and Rollo was so curious he thought he would burst. Katla led them inside, past all the old wooden furniture and dried fish hung in rows. Rollo's pencil drawings from last night were still spread out on the table, and the smoky scent of the fire was strong in the room. Asa helped Katla move the table and roll up the rug under it—to reveal the trapdoor to the Keep itself. They inched down the narrow staircase and found a place in the corner stateroom, where all of King Sigurd's books were stored. Egil sat on the shelving stool. By the light of a flickering candle, the children settled on the chairs next to him, puzzled and hopeful.

Katla bustled in and out, clucking anxiously about the cut on Asa's palm. Worry was etched on her usually smiling round face.

Egil took his time, staring for long seconds—first at Asa, then Rollo. Not even the hint of a smile touched his thin lips, and Rollo had to admit he was frightened of the old man.

"I have searched for you children for nearly a year," he said at last. The candlelight made eerie, shifting shadows on his craggy face. "I was sent by your parents, when they were on their way to . . . their fate."

Rollo felt Asa stiffen next to him. Egil was talking about the night his mother and father were murdered.

"You spoke to them?" Asa said.

Egil nodded once, deeply. "I did."

"What did they say?" Rollo asked.

"I can tell you this: their last thoughts were of you and your sister."

"So Una wasn't with them?" Asa asked. "When they were killed?"

"No. At the last moment, the witch princess Margritt, Flood's half sister who despises him, stole the little babe and took her to her castle in the north."

"Is she well?" Rollo asked. "Can we see her?" He remembered Una's tiny, soft fingers and her sweet, gummy smile. He loved his baby sister so much and thought of her every night when he went to sleep. In his dreams he saw them all—his mother, his father, and Una—as though the flood had never come and his happiness had never been washed away with the mighty tide.

"Silence, child," Egil said sternly. "Listen to the whole tale. It will all become clear.

"I was working as a jailer when Flood first brought your parents in. I suppose Flood thought that a creature like me, so used to living underground at the dungeons in the company of thieves and traitors, would have a heart as black as his own. But he was wrong. King Sigurd was kind to my mother when I was just a babe. Her own family had thrown her out, and we would have starved without his generosity. I grew up believing I owed my life to King Sigurd, and no matter how many gold pieces Flood gave me, my loyalty could not be bought.

"The night before the King and Queen's execution, I slipped into their cell to promise them a final wish. Alas, I could not set them free. After Una's disappearance, Flood's spies were thick near the entrance to the dungeons. So King Sigurd, your father, charged me to seek you out, to tell you about Una, and to give you all you need to find her."

"Find her?" said Rollo. "We have to *find* her?"

"Now listen," Egil said. "And no more interruptions. You know that Flood was once your father's court sorcerer, but did you know there was another? A secret sorcerer named Ragni, whom your father trusted and loved well."

Asa and Rollo exchanged curious glances. They thought they knew everyone who had lived at the Sea Palace before the flood.

"No, I've never heard of him," Rollo said.

Egil nodded, his grim face set hard. "Ragni suspected Flood of mischief, and he put into place some insurance. In case the worst happened—and, as we all know, it did. Do you remember the night of the masked ball?"

Rollo nodded, remembering the great hall of the Sea Palace decorated with shimmering gold and red ribbons. That night, the dukes and duchesses from every principality had come in their fine costumes. Music had echoed around the dark wooden beams and the fires had glowed hot. The magic tricks were marvelous and the ice cream so creamy and sweet that he'd eaten too much. It was the last party before the flood.

"Then you'd remember the magic tricks of the jester? The tall man in blue and gold?"

"The one with the doves?" Asa said,  wincing as Katla cleaned her wound with stinging squid-balm. "He was wonderful. The way he made himself disappear behind that silver cloth!"

"Do you remember that, before he disappeared, he cast upon you three children a cloud of golden dust?"

The children nodded, and Asa said, "The dust stayed in my hair for two days. I couldn't brush it out."

"That magician was Ragni," Egil said. "The dust was enchanted."

"What do you mean?" Rollo said, growing excited. "He *enchanted* us?"

Egil paused for a moment, scratching under his chin. The sound of his fingernails rubbing his beard stubble was loud in the expectant silence.

"Yes," he said at last. "Ragni gave you magic powers."

Asa gasped. Katla dropped the squid-balm and the jar rattled on the cold flagstones.

"What kind of magic powers?" Rollo spluttered.

Egil pointed a bony finger at Asa. "You can change into a raven at will. You only have to close your eyes and say, 'Wings of a raven upon me.'"

Now he pointed at Rollo, who almost couldn't take a breath, he was so excited.

"You can breathe underwater," Egil said. "Close your eyes and say, 'Breath of a fish within me,' and you'll never drown."

Breathe underwater? Unbelievable! Impossible! Wonderful!

"And Una, when she's old enough to speak," Egil continued, "will be able to understand any language, whether it's the language of men or birds or sea giants."

Rollo's heart was bursting. He turned to Asa and saw the gleam in her eyes.

"Can I do it?" she asked. "Can I change into a raven now?"

Egil's eyebrows drew down fiercely and his eyes

almost disappeared under hooded lids. "No. This isn't a game. Use your enchantments only when you absolutely must."

Rollo felt his heart droop. "Why?"

"Because the transformations will make you ill and exhausted. Use them only as a last resort." To Rollo's surprise, Egil got to his feet and straightened his back. "There's one more thing, children. A special present your father charged me with the responsibility of bringing to you."

Rollo scrambled to his feet.

Her hand freshly bandaged, Asa was wary. "What present?"

"Come on. It's down at the inlet."

The two of them looked to Katla and she nodded. "It's all right, children. Follow him."

They returned through the cottage and then down the steep path from Two Hills Keep to the inlet that ran out to the Great Sea. Mist clung to the banks; the early sun hadn't fallen into the valley yet. Katla hung back, under the shade of a water oak. Egil took the children all the way to the edge of the inlet so that they stood on the thin strip of gray sand.

"Do you see it?" he said.

"See what?" said Rollo, peering into the mist.

Egil offered his hand. Rollo took it reluctantly: the old man's fingers were rough and papery. Egil led him a little way up the beach and pointed directly in front of them, where the mist was thickest.

"Can you see it now?" he asked.

"No," Rollo said.

"Good," said Egil, and he smiled mysteriously. He pulled Rollo's hand. "Now take a step."

"A step?" Rollo glanced from Egil's crooked face to the misty water below. "Into the water?"

"What have you to fear? You cannot drown."

"But—"

"Step into the mist," Egil said, pulling harder on his hand. "It's what King Sigurd wanted."

The boy swallowed. Thinking of his father made him brave and he took a step, expecting his foot to hit the water. Instead, it landed on something solid. He looked down and realized he was standing on a gang-plank. Another step into the mist and in front of him, where there'd been nothing before, was a sleek longship.

"How—?"

Egil smiled. "Welcome aboard *Northseeker*."

CHAPTER 3

ABOARD
NORTHSEEKER

"Rollo!" cried Asa. One minute, Rollo held Egil's hand at the edge of the inlet; the next, he had disappeared into the mist.

"Where is he?" she demanded, running to the spot where he had been.

Egil caught her. "It's all right, Asa."

She wrenched herself away from his spidery fingers. "Get your hands off me! Where is my brother?"

"I see you're as spirited as your mother," Egil said, and for the first time he smiled warmly. "Go on, get on board." He shoved her in the direction of the misty water. She cried out, but then her foot struck the gangplank and a longship appeared in front of her. She gasped.

Rollo waited at the top of the gangplank. "Come on, Asa. You have to see this!"

Northseeker was a small version of King Sigurd's own longship. Whereas the King's ship needed twenty men to row it, *Northseeker* was built for two. The boards and beams were all black wood, and a carved dragon's head decorated the prow. Its fiery eyes were inlaid with rubies, its wooden teeth were bared, and its wooden tongue rolled forward. Round shields lined the sides of the boat, painted in royal reds and golds. Its two masts were straight and high, disappearing into the mist above them. The rectangular sails were spun like cobwebs, silvery and light and fluttering in the morning breeze.

Asa pointed at the sails. "How does it sail without cloth?"

23

Egil sat on the gangplank and considered them. "*Northseeker* is a ghost ship," he explained. "Ragni built it from mists and shadows, and it needs no wind to help it move."

Rollo was unwinding ropes and jiggling the carved wooden tiller. "And you can't see it unless you're on it. Is that right?"

"Yes, that's right," said Egil. "You can travel the length and breadth of the sunken kingdom and the sky patrol will never find you. Unless . . ." He held up a cautionary finger. "Unless the rising sun hits the mast. Then, until you are in shadow again, you will be visible."

Asa nodded, easing the tiller from Rollo's hands before he broke it. "So as long as we stay out of the rising sun, we're safe?"

The corner of Egil's mouth twitched downward. "Well, not exactly."

She felt uneasy. "What do you mean?"

"It's a ghost ship, Asa. Men can't see it, nor can women or children. But ghosts can—and any of the other spirits of the deep. And while you're on board, you'll be able to see them. For although it appears you travel in our world, you actually travel in the mist between the worlds. You will see things . . . things that may frighten you."

"It's dangerous, then?" Rollo said. "This journey."

"Ghosts won't bother you unless you bother them. It's still Flood's patrols that are your main concern. If you see a spirit, or a sea giant, just steer away. Fast." He patted the long handle of the tiller.

Rollo indicated two large boxes sitting in the back of the ship. "What are these?"

"Supplies. Food and clothing, for you two and for Una when you rescue her. You'll find maps and compasses, too. But if you become lost, don't worry. Just let the tiller go and *Northseeker* will turn to the north."

Asa leaned over the side of the ship and gazed down at the dark water. Although part of her was frightened by this talk of ghosts and sea giants, another part of her was thrilled by the idea of sailing off in an enchanted ship to find Una. She could hardly believe her baby sister was still alive. It made her heart ache to think about it.

"What do you say, children?" Egil asked, his voice quiet now and respectful. "Will you go?"

Asa looked at Rollo and he nodded firmly. She took a deep breath and reminded herself that she was a princess. Indeed, one day, if Flood's evil was ever defeated, she would be the Star Queen. For these reasons, she should be brave and fulfill her royal duty.

"It was our parents' dying wish that we go," she said. "Thank you, Egil Cripplehand. We'll steer *Northseeker* from here."

She and Rollo went ashore for teary farewells with Aunt Katla, then stepped once more into the mist and away on their adventure. Katla and Egil watched them from the edge of the inlet as the morning sun sloped down into the valley and pierced the mist. The ship was at once visible, then the children steered it into the shadow of the tall cliffs and disappeared from view.

CHAPTER 4

THE SEA HAG

"Can I steer for a while?" Rollo asked.

Asa turned to Rollo with an irritated expression. "I'm the oldest, I should steer," she said for the fifth time. They had left home three hours ago and her fingers hadn't once left the tiller.

"But if I don't learn how to steer now—"

"You keep studying the map."

Rollo glanced down at the map, which was spread

out across his lap. They had found it among a pile of other maps in one of the wooden boxes Egil had left on board. The map was inked in bright blues and yellows and reds, and all of the seaways between Two Hills Keep and Margritt's tower were marked clearly. Rollo estimated they had eight days' sailing ahead of them. If Asa wouldn't let him steer at all, it would be a very boring eight days.

Northseeker moved swift and silent through the water, with magic filling her sails. Rollo opened the second box and began searching.

"Egil's thought of everything," he said, finding a tin of barley biscuits and cracking open the lid. He offered one to Asa, but she shook her head. "Look," he said through a mouthful. "Clothes! Some for me, some for you, and—" He held up a little blue dress. "Isn't this too big for Una?"

Asa glanced at it. "No. Remember, we haven't seen her for a year. She won't be a tiny baby anymore. She'll be walking—maybe even talking."

Rollo folded the dress away and reached for another

barley biscuit. "She's been alive all this time and we didn't know, Asa."

"I can hardly believe it," she said.

"You'll have to believe it when we find her."

"*If* we find her," she said sternly. "We have a long way to go, and Margritt is a witch princess who bears us no love. She's Flood's half sister, and while it's said she hates him, we must still be careful."

"You're so gloomy," Rollo said, and turned to stare out to sea. Asa's dark mood took the shine off his excitement. In the distance, he could see a black rock jutting out of the silver water.

"Maybe I will have one of those barley biscuits after all," Asa whispered.

Rollo turned his attention back to her with a hopeful smile. "Let me steer for a while?"

"Yes, all right. Just a little while." She offered him the tiller and moved out of the way so he could sit down.

Rollo grasped it.

"Now, you pull it *this* way to turn to your right, and *this* way to turn to your left. Got it?"

He pulled it the wrong way.

"No, *this* way," she said patiently. "But don't worry. We're on course at the moment, so just hold it. I'm going to look at those maps."

She sat across from him, pulling all the maps into her lap and sorting through them. Sunlight filtered softly through the mist and gleamed on her dark hair. The ship started veering slightly to the left, and Rollo realized he was holding the tiller too hard. He eased off and they straightened again. The black rock ahead was in the way, so he would have to steer around it as they drew closer.

"There are maps here of the whole sunken kingdom," Asa said, her fingers tracing across them. "All the towers that are still above water and all those that are submerged. Egil must have drawn these while he was searching for us."

Rollo peered down at the maps. Asa snapped her head up and said, "Are you watching where we're going?"

"Yes," he said quickly, looking out to sea again. The

black rock was gone. Puzzled, he glanced around.

"That's odd," he said.

"What's odd?"

Then, with water streaming off it, the rock thrust itself above the surface, just a few feet from their bow.

"Asa!" Rollo cried, yanking on the tiller.

She dropped the map. "Other way, Rollo!"

"It's not working."

A gray shape on the rock moved and Rollo's blood turned to ice. It was a sea hag, her wizened face staring at them skull-like under seaweed hair. She pointed a long, bony finger at him and bared her teeth. Hissing, she turned her hand over and crooked her finger. "Come!" she called in a rasping voice.

Rollo's heart thundered. Asa flung herself over him and grabbed the tiller.

"She's jammed it!" she yelled.

The sea hag scrambled like a lizard across the rock to the edge of the water, with her hand stretched out. "Come! Come!" They were almost close enough to touch.

Rollo suddenly remembered something Egil had told them. "Let it go!" He threw himself onto Asa and pushed her fingers off the tiller. "If we let the tiller go, the ship will turn to the north."

Asa let go and fell onto her back in the bottom of the ship.

As the sea hag's fingers grasped at *Northseeker*'s side, her claws dug into the wood and held fast. "Come on, tasty little ones," she said, her voice like broken glass.

Asa screamed. The hag began to pull the ship toward her.

But there was a long creaking noise as *Northseeker* strained away. If the hag's magic was stronger than the ship's, then Asa and Rollo would be on her watery table for dinner.

There was a horrible scratching noise as the hag's claws began to drag through the wood. She snarled.

And *Northseeker* turned.

The hag was flung off and two of her claws were left

embedded in the wood. The ship picked up speed, skimming past the black rock and out into open water. Behind them, there was a splash.

"She's following us," Asa said. "Hurry, *Northseeker!*"

Rollo glanced behind him. The hag was in the water, squealing and wet and propelling herself forward with her wiry arms.

"Row," he yelled, grabbing one of the big oars that were stored in the side of the ship.

Asa dived at the other oar and they began to pull hard. The ship picked up speed, but the hag was still closing in on them and her bloodied hand touched the side.

Asa leapt to her feet, raised her oar above her, and brought it crashing down on the sea hag's head. There was a sickening thud and the hag let go. *Northseeker,* regaining her strength and filling her sails with magic, pulled away fast, until the hag was just a dark shape in the shining sea, disappearing behind them.

As Asa took her seat again and caught her breath,

Rollo picked the sea hag's claws out of the wood. They sat on his palm, sharp and yellowed, and he felt just how lucky they'd been to escape her.

"You're right, Asa," he said. "We have to be careful."

"You were right, too," she said. "If I'd let you steer earlier, you'd have known what to do." She brought the ship back on course and offered him the tiller. "From now on, we take turns."

CHAPTER 5

WINGS OF A RAVEN, BREATH OF A FISH

They anchored each evening to eat and sleep, but were away each morning before sunrise, clinging to the shadows of cliffs and valleys. Day after day *Northseeker* sailed on, her cobweb sails fluttering in the mist, while they grew homesick for Katla's rabbit stew and their own warm beds.

Before their journey, Asa hadn't seen what had become of the Star Lands beyond the fields and beaches around the Keep. Katla's house was a long way from anywhere out there, on the very last island before the Great Sea, where Flood rarely turned his gaze. Now the ship was carrying them through the heart of the sunken kingdom. Here, there had once been bustling cities, mighty towers, and broad farmlands. Since the flood, whole cities had been submerged, and villages had sprouted on hilltops and cliff edges. Occasionally, they passed a cathedral spire poking out of the water, or sailed over barely submerged turrets. Once, Asa saw the black shape of a sea giant in the shadowy depths of a drowned castle. She held her breath until *Northseeker* had sped them safely away between green farmhills.

No one saw the ship, but Asa and Rollo saw everyone: the farmer coaxing his cow out of the mud at the edge of the water; the village witch collecting her secret herbs at the foot of a sea willow; the children trudging up the hill with a lineful of fish to dry. Farther north, the air grew colder and they searched in the bottom of Egil's wooden trunks for heavy cloaks of bearskin. The cliffs grew darker and rockier, and here and there the water was streaked with ice. They were nearing the tower of the witch princess. Late in the afternoon, two enormous cliffs loomed ahead of them— the passage between them narrow and dark.

"Which way?" Rollo said.

Asa studied the map. "Straight through."

Rollo looked up at the cliffs, dizzyingly high on either side. The crumbling edges jutted out and almost met at the top. Even *Northseeker* slowed, as though she were wary.

"Do you think it's safe?" Rollo asked. "Those rocks look loose."

Asa's eyes scanned the map nervously. She didn't want to go through the narrow passage, either. Egil's map had made it look like an easy course, and it was certainly the most direct. Then, as if to confirm her fears, a shower of loose stones freed themselves from the cliff face and peppered the water. She turned the map around to show Rollo.

"You see? If we want to avoid these cliffs, we'll have to sail back the way we came"—she indicated the

course with her finger—"then hook around this island here. Egil has marked it as a bay full of sea giants."

"Or we could go this way," Rollo said, pointing out a different route.

"That would add nearly six days to our trip."

They gazed at each other. *Northseeker,* sensing their indecision, had come to a standstill.

"What should we do?" Rollo asked.

"I don't know."

"But you always know what to do," he said.

"Well, I don't this time."

"Sea giants, or another six days on board, or between the cliffs?"

Asa gazed up at the cliffs again. A sea wind howled through the passage, buffeting the ship and stinging her eyes with cold. On the other side, just a day's sail away, was her baby sister.

"Let's go through," she said.

Rollo smiled. "That's just what I was going to say."

They picked up speed and, laying the map out on the seat beside her, Asa took the tiller. "I'll watch the east cliff; you watch the west one. If any rocks and stones come loose, we'll try to steer around them."

"Got it," he said, turning his face up to the east cliff.

"Other one, Rollo."

"Got it," he said, studying the west cliff.

Asa lined the ship up and willed her to move fast through the passage. It narrowed ahead of her and *Northseeker* slowed again.

"Why are we going so slowly?" Rollo asked.

Asa peered over the side. "Rocks," she said. "The cliffs continue under the water, and the ship is avoiding the reef." She pointed ahead, just on the other side of the passage, where the water was deep and blue. "The reef drops off there, so we'll be safe again."

"On the other side."

"Yes. On the other side."

Asa concentrated hard, her eyes flicking from the reef to the arch of the cliffs above them. A scatter of small pebbles rolled down the cliff and echoed loudly. *Northseeker* was about to pass directly under the two jutting edges.

"Asa," Rollo said quietly.

"What?"

"Do you see it?"

She strained her eyes. "Yes," she said, her lungs filling with fear. A crack appeared in the edge of the western cliff.

"*Northseeker*, we have to go faster," Asa said.

But the ship kept her pace and scraped lightly over a rocky protrusion.

Creak.

"It's going to fall," Rollo said, holding his breath.

Creeeeeeeak. The crack split, the rock dropped a fraction, then held. A shower of dust descended on them. *Crack!*

Asa shrieked. A huge rock, easily the size of the ship itself, was plummeting directly toward them.

Northseeker jerked forward, bumping Asa off her seat. The map next to her fluttered. The rock landed with a huge crash, barely an inch from the stern of the longship, and soaked them with icy water as they squeezed through the passage. The longship bobbed free of the reef. Just when Asa thought they were perfectly safe and that nothing else bad could happen, a howling wind raced through the passage and ripped the map skyward.

The map hovered above her for a half second. She reached for it, but accidentally knocked it farther away. Then the wind suddenly died and the map fell into the water.

"Oh no!" She raced to the side of the ship and watched the map sink down into the icy blue.

Rollo joined her. "Do we still need it?" he said. "You've been poring over it ever since we left home. You know the way, don't you?"

She shook her head. "Around the next island, there's a bay with lots of shallow water and the course gets very complex. If I don't know which way to take, we could run aground, or even tear a hole in the ship."

Safe once again in deep water, *Northseeker* slowed to a halt.

"We have to get the map back, then," Rollo said, shrugging out of his fur cloak.

"What are you doing?"

"Going to get the map."

"But it's too deep. You'll drown."

Rollo grinned. "No. I can breathe underwater, remember?"

"But, Rollo—"

"Breath of a fish within me," he shouted, and dived over the side of the longship.

"Rollo, no!" She peered over the side into the water. He had disappeared from sight. How long should she wait before she panicked? One minute? Two? What if the enchantment didn't work? It was deep here, and dark and cold. Two minutes passed. Asa gnawed on her thumbnail and watched.

"Come on, Rollo, come on," she muttered.

A moment later, he surfaced,

clutching the map and laughing.

She reached down to help him back on board. "Did you do it? Did you breathe underwater?" she asked.

"Asa, it felt amazing!" he shouted.

She reached for a cloth to dry him off. "Wasn't it cold?"

"Not at all. I felt like a fish. And I could see *Northseeker* the whole time." He pulled his fur cloak back on. "I don't feel ill or tired, despite what Egil said."

Asa was thinking. How she longed to try out her special magic, too.

"Asa?"

She smiled at him, then closed her eyes and threw open her arms. "Wings of a raven upon me!"

What a sensation! Her shoulders hunching together, her bones and muscles contracting, her fingers elongating and growing light. Her chest tightened, but it wasn't painful. A feeling of weightlessness gripped her and she flung out her arms to find they were actually black wings.

She took to the sky.

A giddy rush as the air surrounded her and she shot out of the cloud of mist around *Northseeker* and into the pale blue sky. She tried to laugh, but only a raven's caw came out and, watching the clouds spin above her, she dipped and dived on the wind.

And then there was something else. Something black and hissing. A sky patrol.

Her blood turned to ice.

She dropped down and back to *Northseeker,* but the balloon was moving fast and gaining on her from behind. Her tiny bird's heart began to beat in a panic as she plummeted through the sky.

Sssshhhhhhhhhhhhhhhhhhhh.

The mists parted around her and she was back on *Northseeker.* She let her breath go and her wings dissolved. Her own body, feeling heavy and stiff, gathered around her once more.

"Sky patrol," she gasped.

Rollo was staring at her. "That was amazing!"

"Sky patrol, Rollo!" She wondered why he wasn't panicking.

Rollo turned his face upward. The balloon was directly overhead now. "Why are you worried, Asa?" he said. "They can't see us."

Of course. Why hadn't she thought of it? She was so used to hiding when she saw one of the dark balloons, but *Northseeker* was invisible. She began to laugh, with relief and with the thrill of having changed into a bird.

Rollo laughed, too, and then poked his tongue out at the balloon. "You can't see us," he teased in a sing-song voice. She joined in, and they laughed until the sky patrol had gone ahead, over the cliffs and into the distance.

"I don't feel ill at all," she said. "Maybe Egil was making it up."

"Probably trying to scare us," said Rollo. "Trying to stop us having any fun at all so we're just as miserable as him."

She agreed and they kept sailing.

But by nightfall, after sailing the twisted course between the islands, she was feeling distinctly queasy.

"I don't think I can sit up any longer," she said.

Rollo was picking at his plate of cheese and pickled fish. "I feel sick."

"And exhausted," she added. "Like my arms and legs weigh a ton."

"It hurts to breathe. Like my ribs are bruised," he groaned.

"This is what Egil meant, isn't it? We're sick because we used our magic powers."

"I think I'm going to—" Rollo was suddenly on his feet, leaning over the side of the ship and throwing up.

Asa steered into the shelter of a bay and dropped anchor. They were so close to Margritt's tower, but they weren't going to make it tonight. Even though it was early, they would have to sleep.

Asa laid the bearskin in the bottom of the longship and Rollo snuggled next to her.

"I feel terrible," he said.

"A good night's sleep will help," she said, pulling the

blankets over them. She closed her eyes and tried to fight the queasy feeling.

"Do you regret it, though?" Rollo said.

Asa was just on the edge of sleep, and smiled. Regret turning herself into a bird and feeling those magical sensations? Never. "No," she said.

"Nor do I."

And they both fell into a deep slumber.

So it wasn't until early morning, with the low line of an island to shadow them, that they sailed into sight of a thin black spire on the horizon. Dark clouds gathered around it and the water was black beneath it.

Rollo frowned. "That looks creepy."

"It's Margritt's tower," Asa said. "We've arrived."

CHAPTER 6

THE TOWER OF THE WITCH PRINCESS

Margritt's tower had once been the finest tower in the north. Even though the base was now half submerged, the tall peak still rose higher than the ragged black cliffs around it. *Northseeker* came to rest against a narrow spine of stairs that wrapped around the tower. Asa could see the stairs continued deep under the water and wound high up above them. An icy wind chafed her face as she measured the distance upward with her eyes.

"Is that the only way in?" Rollo asked.

"Unless you want to go under the water."

He smiled. "I could."

"But I couldn't. And we have to stick together."

She grabbed his hand and they left *Northseeker* behind. The stairs were slimy with algae and there was no railing to hold on to, so they picked their way up carefully. Above, Asa could see a collar around the tower. It had once been a bulwark, but now it was the entrance.

"That's where we're going," Asa said, pointing.

"Will they let us in?"

"I hope so. Egil Cripplehand said that we had to ask for Margritt and to say we were friends of his. No matter what happens, don't tell anyone we're the Star Queen's children. We don't know who we can trust."

He nodded and they continued up the narrow stairs. Asa's heart was thumping, from the effort of climbing as much as from excitement. Somewhere in this tower, according to Egil, was their baby sister.

Finally, they reached the bulwark. It was now a

wide, muddy courtyard. Once they were on level ground, Asa and Rollo found their way barred by a heavy iron gate lined with spikes. Beyond it, they could see a cobbled path and men in long, hooded cloaks moving around in a stony garden.

"Hello?" Rollo called. "Hello?"

One of the hooded men turned to them. His face was in shadow.

"We're here to see Margritt," Asa said.

The man approached the gate. "Who are you?"

"Friends of Egil Cripplehand." Asa was careful not to admit to her true identity. "Can you tell her we're here?"

"Wait," he said, then crossed the courtyard and disappeared.

An hour passed, then another, and Asa started to think they had been forgotten. Rollo sat on the muddy ground drawing pictures with a stick, and Asa paced. They were so close to Una now. She couldn't bear this long wait.

Finally, the hooded man (or another—they all

looked the same) opened the gate without a word and led them through. A twisted black tree, bare of leaves, stood in the center of the courtyard. Ugly carved gargoyles crouched on the corners, their evil eyes and sharp stone teeth decorated with spiderwebs. Asa and Rollo entered a long, low hallway, where only the faintest glow from a lamp lit the way.

"Go right to the end and wait," the man said, and left them.

Asa's heart fluttered. Rollo reached for her hand and they walked the long corridor in silence.

"There are a lot of spiders in this place," he said.

She glanced around. He was right. Every corner was spun with webs. It made her flesh crawl. A particularly large spider sat on the highest point of a nearby arch and Asa could have sworn it was looking at her. "I've never much liked spiders," she said.

"Maybe you'd feel differently if you changed into a raven," Rollo said cheerfully. "Some birds eat spiders, don't they?"

"Well, I know I'm not a spider-eating bird."

"You might be. Mmmmm," he said, rubbing his tummy. "Tasty spiders."

"I'm not! I'd never eat spiders."

Rollo wrinkled his nose at her. "Hey, it's a joke. I'm only trying to cheer you up."

"There's nothing cheerful about this situation, Rollo," she said. "It's no time for jokes." She immediately regretted having snapped at him. "I'm sorry. I'm just so tense and I want to see Una and go home safely."

Rollo squeezed her hand. "We'll be fine. You'll see."

Ahead at the end of the hall, a heavy wooden door stained with mold waited for them.

Rollo took a deep breath. "We'll see her soon, won't we?"

"I hope so."

He opened the door and they found themselves in a dim room. The stone floor was bare and cold, and flickering candles hung in rusted iron brackets on the walls. A fire burned in the grate and a plump servant stood in front of it, boiling water. An uneven wooden table and two chairs with torn covers had been set up near the fire. Only a narrow window let in a little light. Firelit shadows danced on the walls.

"Hello?" Asa said.

The servant turned. At first she had a smile on her lips, but when she saw them, her expression changed. She only had one eye and she narrowed it at them suspiciously. "*You're* the guests?"

"I . . . I suppose so," Asa said.

"Margritt told me to bathe you and feed you." She came closer, trying to make them out with her one eye. Her nose wrinkled. "I'm Hallgird."

"Very pleased to meet you," Rollo said, though he probably didn't mean it.

"What are your names?" she said.

"How long before we can see Margritt?" Asa carefully avoided introducing herself.

"I said, what are your names?" Hallgird demanded.

"We're friends of Egil Cripplehand," Rollo said smoothly.

"We'll only answer questions from Margritt," Asa said.

Hallgird picked up Asa's hands in her own sweaty fingers and spread her arms apart. She considered Asa in the gloomy light, the pupil in her glassy eye narrowed to a pinpoint. "You look familiar."

"I'm sure I don't, because we've never met." Asa pulled her hands away. "Where is Margritt?"

Hallgird huffed and turned her shoulder. "She'll be along in her own time. Sit down, eat. Then I'll draw you a bath."

She served them a plate of limp vegetables, then filled a bath with the same water she had boiled the food in. Asa smelled like a carrot afterward, and the food didn't sit well in her still-queasy stomach. Hours and hours passed. Asa paced; Rollo watched the fire. Hallgird bustled in and out, and so did other servants, who were friendlier and gentler with them. But nobody would tell them where Margritt was or when she would come. Outside the narrow window, the sun grew low in the sky again, and Asa began to give up hope. Margritt wouldn't come. Una wasn't here. Their journey had been in vain.

"Cheer up," Rollo said, smiling at her. "We'll see Una soon."

"What if we don't? What if we—"

At that precise moment, the door creaked open and a long shadow crossed the threshold ahead of a tall, thin woman. In a self-important voice, she dismissed all the servants, including a wary-eyed Hallgird.

"Quickly now," Margritt said, clapping her hands together. "Out, out! I want to speak to my guests in private. You, too, Hallgird. I'll call if I need you. Make sure Nanny Freya is told of my plans."

When they were alone, she closed the door carefully behind her and turned to consider the children.

Margritt was striking, with raven-black hair pulled away from her face and trailing in a long sweep at her back. Woven among the black strands of her hair were hundreds of tiny star-shaped diamonds. Her eyes were icy blue and her mouth turned down sharply. In the candlelight, dark shadows flickered across her face and made her look hard. Her robes were black and she wore a collar of spiderweb lace around her throat. Every

finger bore a glittering ring and they flashed as she moved her hands.

"Asa? Rollo?" she said at last, her face expressionless.

Asa smiled, extending her hand. "We're so grateful to—"

"Hush!" Margritt said sharply. "I'm not your friend. I hated your parents, but I hated my half brother more. It's the only reason I did what I did. I suppose you want to see your sister?"

So Una really was alive! Asa was so overwhelmed she couldn't speak.

"Please, ma'am," Rollo said respectfully, "we want to take her home with us."

Margritt arched her eyebrows. "And what will you give me in return? As payment?"

Asa found her voice. "Payment?"

"You don't think I'm just going to hand her over. If she's worth something to you, you'll pay me."

"She's our sister!" Rollo cried angrily. "We've traveled for days and days and—"

Asa touched his shoulder. "No, Rollo. Don't argue."

She turned to Margritt. "What do you want?"

Margritt flicked her long ponytail over her shoulder. "I'm quite fond of diamonds."

Asa looked down at her own hands. They were worn and callused from managing the ship's tiller, and that cut still hadn't healed properly. She wore a little gold ring her father had given her for her ninth birthday, three years ago. As she had grown, she had moved it along from one finger to the next. Her smallest finger was the last place it would fit. Nestled in the center of the ring was a round diamond.

"But Papa gave you that." Rollo had guessed what Asa was thinking.

She pulled the ring off and held it out to Margritt. "Will this do?"

Margritt plucked the ring from Asa's palm. She strode to the nearest candle, held it close to the flame, and examined it carefully. At first her mouth turned down, but then it broke into a smile.

She turned to Asa. "It's a Great Sea Diamond."

"Yes, found under the rocks at the Deeps." Asa

remembered her father telling her that he had found the diamond himself while diving to rescue his brother from a sea giant. How she had loved the story, and how she had loved the gift. It hurt her to have to give it up. "It's rare," she said. "It's priceless."

Margritt's fingers snapped shut around the ring. "It will do nicely, then. I'll fetch the child for you." Her nose wrinkled. "I had a mind to train her as a witch's apprentice, but she's a noisy, smelly little thing."

The witch princess went to the door and threw it open. An elderly nanny with a kind face stood there. In one arm, she held a brown paper package. In the other, she held a squirming infant.

Asa would have recognized the little girl anywhere: she had her mother's piercing green eyes and her father's gentle smile.

"Una!"

She and Rollo descended upon the little girl, who cried at first but then soon warmed to the tearful cuddles and kisses. Una couldn't speak yet, but her delighted giggles said exactly what she was feeling. Asa couldn't remember a nicer sensation than the tender contentment of holding her baby sister in her arms at last. It made her feel whole.

"You had best spend the night here and set off in the morning," Margritt said when calm had returned. "Hallgird will fix you some supper and show you the way."

The one-eyed servant entered the room and smiled knowingly at Asa. She felt a worm of discomfort. What had Hallgird overheard?

Their bedchamber was a drafty room of gloomy corners cluttered with all manner of carved monsters and thick spiderwebs. Hallgird served them more limp vegetables (cold this time) for supper, but neither Asa nor Rollo could concentrate on eating. After Hallgird had left, they all flopped on the big four-poster bed together. Rollo tickled Una, who laughed and squealed happily. Asa picked the string off the brown paper package.

"Can you say anything, Una?" Rollo asked.

"Gaaaaaaaah!" she said happily.

"Why doesn't she know any words?" he said.

"Perhaps nobody has taught her any." Asa opened the package. Inside were the clothes Una had been wearing the night she was stolen. Also a little book, a cotton rabbit . . . she sorted through them all, Una's belongings from before the flood.

Rollo bent over their baby sister. "Can you say Rollo? *Rol-lo?*" he said slowly.

"Aaaawoo!" she said.

"Did you hear that, Asa? I think she's trying to say my name."

Asa gasped as her fingers turned over the last item in the package: a little pair of white knitted socks. Something shiny had dropped out.

"Oh, Asa," Rollo said, picking it up. "Do you remember this?"

"The Moonstone Star," she said, and her face lit up. "It's Mama's. The royal symbol of the Star Lands, and it's full of magic."

Rollo caressed the Star gently. "She wore it all the time."

His eyes brimmed with tears and Asa ruffled his hair.

"Imagine," she said. "Margritt fussed so much over that diamond, when a far greater treasure has been here under her nose the whole time." She took the Star from Rollo and tucked it once again into the little white sock. "I guess moonstone isn't shiny enough for her."

Rollo turned his attention once again to Una, but she had fallen asleep.

"She must be tired," he said.

Asa nudged him. "I'm tired, too," she said.

"I don't know if I can sleep in this creepy place," Rollo said, slipping into the bed next to his sisters.

"Me neither," Asa said, nervously eyeing the cob-webs. "Do you think the spiders might crawl on us in the night?"

He wriggled closer, so that their knees were touching. There was Una on her back between them, her soft little face turned to the right, her lips parted. "Perhaps if we all snuggle up really close, everything will be fine," he said.

He was right. Once the three of them were curled

up tightly together, the warmth of family seemed much stronger than the cold kiss of shadows. Sleep came, soft and restful.

But outside, on the muddy stairs, Hallgird was doing her best to bring the shadows closing in.

CHAPTER 7

RETURN TO
TWO HILLS KEEP

Rollo woke to a hiss.

His eyes flew open. *Sky patrol!*

"Asa?"

But she was already scrambling out of bed, clutching Una to her chest and throwing open the shutters.

"It's a balloon and it's landed behind the tower. We have to run," Asa told him.

They turned as the door to their chamber was flung open. Hallgird blocked their path.

"Don't leave so soon," she said, breaking into a wicked smile. Her single eye crinkled up in delight. "Not when you have visitors."

"Why did you call them?" Asa demanded. In her arms, Una was babbling more of her nonsensical baby talk.

"Because Flood has set a reward for your capture. The royal children are worth a thousand gold coins each." Hallgird indicated Una. "If I'd known who the baby was, I would have handed her over months ago."

Una kept babbling and Rollo wished she would shush. He couldn't think straight and he had to work out how to get past Hallgird so they could escape to *Northseeker.*

Then there was an odd scuttling sound and a shadow moved above him.

Spiders!

Thousands of them, pouring in through the

windows, from the cracks in the walls, gathering around them. What was going on?

The first one landed on Hallgird's head. She shrieked and tried to brush it off. Then they began to rain down on her, a black skittering, scuttling cloud of spiders.

"Run!" Asa called, and they dashed past Hallgird and the river of spiders out into the corridor.

"What happened?" Rollo asked, glancing back over his shoulder.

"Una," she shouted. "I bet it was her. She may not be able to talk to us yet, but it seems she can talk to spiders."

They ran back the way they had come the previous day, only to find that the heavy gate was closed.

"No!" cried Rollo, shaking it so that it rattled dully.

Asa had backed up a few paces. "Here," she said. "This rope, help me pull it."

She put Una down and they pulled on the rope as hard as they could. Gradually, the gate began to rise.

"I'll hold it while you and Una slide under," Rollo said.

Asa grabbed Una and slipped under the gate.

"Now you," Asa called.

He looked at the rope, which ran over a pulley. The second he let it go the gate would fall. But if he didn't let it go, he couldn't get out. On the stone wall, a single jutting rock caught his eye. He wrapped the rope around it, tied a tight knot, crossed his fingers, and started to run.

The knot slipped. The gate started to descend.

He doubled his speed, sliding to fit underneath.

Slam! Just as he made it through, the gate crashed to the ground and took the hem of his shirt with it. Asa grabbed his hand and they ran for the stairs.

The stairs were slippery and they had to slow down to prevent themselves from falling, and by this time, Una was upset and crying. With one hand stretched out to the damp wall of the tower to steady herself, Asa tried to quiet her.

Rollo followed close behind, conscious that they had to hurry. Were Flood's spies behind them on foot? Or had they realized the children were gone and decided to take to the skies after them once more?

Sssshhhhhhhhhhhhhhhhhhhhh.

His answer came in the horrible hiss of evil lungs. Rollo and Asa wound around the tower and the bottom of the stairs came into view. The rising sun just above the cliffs shot beams of light across the sea and one of them caught *Northseeker*'s mast. She was visible.

"Oh no!" cried Asa.

"Quick," Rollo said. "We have to get her into the shadows."

They half ran, half slid down the muddy bottom stairs. There was a malevolent hiss as the top of the balloon appeared behind the tower. Asa pushed Una on board ahead of her and the little girl began to wail. Rollo hauled on the anchor and they set off, hearts pounding, and steered for the shadow of the cliff.

Sssshhhhhhhhhhhhhhhhhhhhh.

There it was, a huge balloon directly above them. *Northseeker*'s mast gleamed orange in the sun, then suddenly grayed as they disappeared into darkness.

"We did it!" Rollo shouted. "We got away!"

Asa looked serious and pointed at the balloon. "She didn't."

Rollo looked up. Margritt was on board, her hands tied behind her while Flood's spies gripped her arms tightly. Two spies hung from the balloon and turned their brass telescopes in all directions, mystified by the disappearance of the longship.

Rollo couldn't take his eyes off Margritt. She was screaming at her captors and shaking her head.

"We have to rescue her," he said. "She helped us, she—"

"We can't rescue everyone. I'm sorry," Asa said, turning the tiller for home. "Now we have to get Una back safely."

Sick with guilt, Rollo watched the balloon disappear into the sky.

Rollo's own warm bed at Two Hills Keep was the best place in the world, especially with the sound of little Una breathing gently in the cot next to him. Katla tucked him in and kissed his forehead, and he had never been so glad to be home.

"Thank the stars that you two are home safely," Katla said, sitting on the edge of his bed. "The cottage was so empty without you at night."

"We had such an adventure, Aunt Katla," Rollo said. "*Northseeker* is fantastic!"

"Well, let's just hope that Egil Cripplehand comes back for his longship soon."

"I hope he *never* comes back," Rollo said, disappointed as he realized that they might not be able to keep the ship. "I thought *Northseeker* was a gift—to us. From our father."

"I won't have you going away again, Rollo," Katla said, a look of concern furrowing her brow. "I'm keeping you safe here with me."

Asa sat up in bed and gazed at the Moonstone Star, which lay there in her hands.

"Time for sleep now, Asa," Katla whispered.

"What shall I do with it, Aunt Katla?" Asa asked, holding out the Star.

Katla considered her answer for a long time. Finally, she said, "With your mother gone, you are the Star Queen. I know that you have no lands to rule now. But perhaps you should wear it, as your mother did."

Asa shook her head. "I couldn't."

"Yes, you could," Rollo said.

"I . . ." Asa gazed at the Star sadly. "I'm no queen. I'm just a girl."

Katla rose and moved across the room to her bed. "Then let me keep it safe for you, until you are grown."

Reluctantly, Asa let the Star slip into her hand. "Yes. Maybe in a year or two . . ."

"I'll store it with our other treasures, in the Keep."

"No," Rollo said, sitting up. "Don't lock it away down there. Let's hang it over the fireplace so we can think of Mama every day."

"I already think of Mama every day," Asa said softly. "It'll be safer locked away."

"Please, please." Rollo pressed his lips together hard so that he wouldn't cry. "Asa, I'm starting to forget her. I'm starting to forget what she looked like and how her voice sounded and how her hair smelled when she'd just washed it. But when I see the Star, I can remember."

Asa looked across the room at him and her face softened. "Of course. Let's hang it over the fireplace."

Katla smiled and nodded. "I'll do it tonight. Now— time for sleep." She picked up the candle and left, whispering, "Sweet dreams," behind her.

Rollo lay down and closed his eyes. *Sweet dreams.* He knew exactly what he'd dream of tonight.

Once he'd thought that Una was dead, but she wasn't. If she was alive, King Sigurd and the Star Queen might be alive, too.

He closed his eyes and dreamed of finding their parents.

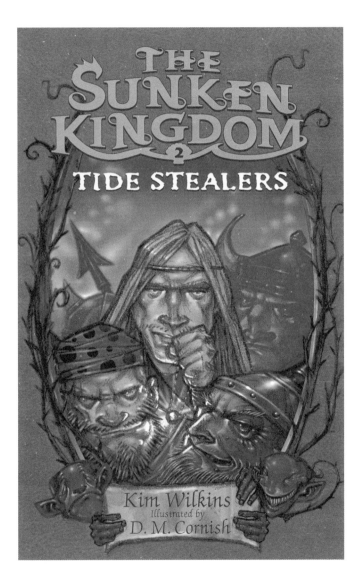

THE SUNKEN KINGDOM

2

TIDE STEALERS

Kim Wilkins

Illustrated by

D. M. Cornish

Asa and Rollo's adventures continue in . . .

THE SUNKEN KINGDOM
BOOK TWO

TIDE STEALERS

The water split open four feet in front of Asa and a longship heaved out! It was wooden, black with algae. Water poured off its bow, seaweed streamed behind it. This was no little fish: this was a band of tide stealers. Asa screamed and jumped backward. Seventeen men were crowded onto the boat. Their faces were dark, their teeth crooked, their clothes wet. The leader, a brawny man with a circlet of gold on his head, pointed to the Moonstone Star.

"Give it to me!" he shouted.

ABOUT THE AUTHOR

Since the publication of her first novel, *The Infernal*, in 1997, Kim Wilkins has established herself as a leading fantasy author in Australia and internationally. Her books include *Grimoire*, *The Resurrectionists*, *Angel of Ruin*, *The Autumn Castle,* and *Giants of the Frost.* She has also written a series for young adults about a psychic detective. She lives in Brisbane, Australia.

Kim's first novel, *The Infernal,* won both the horror and fantasy novel categories of the Aurealis Awards in 1997.

ABOUT THE ILLUSTRATOR

After graduating from the University of South Australia, David Cornish took his portfolio to Sydney, where he found work with several magazines and newspapers. Three years later, an opportunity arose there to be on the drawing team of the game show *Burgo's Catchphrase*. After six years with the show, David became restless, circumnavigating the globe before returning to Adelaide, Australia.

David's bold, graphic style and fine draftsmanship have made him a successful illustrator in Australia, and in the United States he is best known as both the author and the illustrator of the fantasy series Monster Blood Tattoo.

THE SUNKEN KINGDOM